JACOB

BY

HEIDI LOUISE WILLIAMS

Gem-in-Eye Publishing

WARNING: 16+

All rights reserved: No part of this publication may be transmitted or reproduced by any means, electronic, mechanical, photocopying or otherwise without prior permission of the publisher.

First published 2021

Gem-in-Eye Publishing

JACOB

Text copyright © 2021 Heidi Louise Williams

ISBN 9781914996047

Copyright © Heidi Louise Williams

Front cover photo by Charles Deluvio

Original pre-Photoshop internal photo of mother and baby by Zach Lucero

All Characters and events in this book, other than those clearly in the public domain, are fictitious and any resemblance to real persons, being alive or dead is purely coincidental.

CHAPTER ONE

Veronica could see their mouths moving but their words became distorted before they reached her ears. She could feel people touch her hands; some clasped her in their embrace. She wished they would stop touching her. She wished they would all go home. None of this was making her any feel better – it was making it a thousand times worse.

She was expected to put on a brave face, smile and say thank you for coming - to make them feel better. They were not here for her. They did not want to see the raw anguish of her pain. They were there to make themselves feel better, get sympathy for their sadness, to socialise and eat the sandwiches and hope that she would tell them that it was okay, that even this you could survive.

She wished they would all just fuck off.

Maybe she should tell them that. She should just turn off the sombre music that made her chest feel like it was melting, stand in the middle of the room, and dislodge the lump in her throat by screaming, GET OUT OF MY HOUSE!

Instead, she quietly slipped away upstairs, laid down on her bed, and fell asleep.

Half an hour later, she was woken by her mother shaking her.

'Veronica, get up. You are being very rude! You have a house full of people who are here to support you. Wake up, put on a brave face, and go downstairs and entertain your guests,' her mother insisted. Veronica picked up the bedside lamp and threw it in her mother's direction. It smashed against the wall.

Jacqueline Thomas scurried from the room and shut the door, fuming. Now that Vero was being uncivil and wallowing in self-pity, she would have to play the hostess, and hadn't she also lost her grandchild.

JACOB

Veronica curled up in a ball, feeling like her womb had been torn from her body. She did not move out of that position for four days. Her mother tried to force her to eat and drink but Veronica remained unmoving, not hungry, not thirsty, not caring. She just wanted to be left alone. She just wanted to die.

In the days following the funeral, Christine Mathews, best friend and confidant of Veronica Thomas, had been turned away at the door by Veronica's mother. At the end of the week, Christine forced her way in. She found Veronica dishevelled, still lying in a foetal position. She knelt down by the bed, and stroked her friend's hair.

'It's me, Vero.' Veronica opened her eyes and forced a weak smile.

'Come Vero, let's get you into the shower and you will feel better.'

Veronica allowed Christine to help her get up and guide her to the bathroom. Christine helped her to remove her T-shirt and step out of her knickers. Veronica climbed into the bath and sat down, feeling too weak to stand.

Christine unhooked the shower, checked the temperature of the water, and gently washed her friend's stink off her. She washed her hair and scrubbed her back, soaped and rinsed her, then dried her, and helped her into a clean pair of pyjamas.

Veronica sat in a chair while her dear friend changed her sheets. Once Veronica was back into a nice clean bed, Christine carried the bundle of dirty sheets down to the kitchen with the promise of returning with something to eat. She assumed as Veronica had not eaten for almost a week that her stomach might have shrunk, so she made Vero tinned tomato soup that she found in the cupboard, served with two slices of bread and some grapes from the fridge. Veronica's mother stayed out of the way.

Veronica sat up to eat her soup. She felt slightly recharged from the shower and her friend's company. Veronica didn't eat the bread but drank all the soup and nibbled on the grapes. The shower and the food gave her the strength to talk.

'I can't do this, Chris! I just can't live without him! I can't live without my heart,' Veronica admitted to her friend. 'It hurts too much. I can't breathe!'

JACOB

'It will take a lot of time, Vero, but eventually you will learn to live with it.'

'I don't want to! I just want to die!'

'You feel like that now but one day it won't feel as intense. Have you seen Sean?'

'No! I think he has been here but the doctor prescribed me sedatives, and I have been asleep most of the time,' Veronica replied.

'I will go and check on him on my way home. Do you want me to tell him to come over?'

'No! I can't look at him! I don't want to see his face which will just remind me of Jacob.'

'Sean needs you, Vero. He is going through just as much pain as you are. Maybe you can help each other get through this.'

'Jacob did not come from his body! He did not carry him inside his womb for almost ten months! Of course he suffers, he's lost his son, but it is not the same and I can't expect him to understand that,' Veronica answered angrily. 'I need you to leave now. I am so tired. I need to sleep. If I stay awake I will top myself. Seriously, Chris, I can't live without Jacob!' Veronica curled up into ball again and refused to say another word. Christine pulled the duvet up over her friend's thin body, kissed her on the head, and left quietly.

CHAPTER TWO

Veronica was still awake, staring up at the ceiling, when her bedroom door opened and Sean popped his head in to see how she was.

'Oh good, you are awake. I missed you, but every time I came round you were sleeping. I didn't want to disturb you because sleep is precious right now, and personally I can't get any,' Sean said, coming into the room, and spooning her on the bed. It was nice to feel his strong arms holding her, and even better that he was behind her so that she did not have to see the face that reminded her so much of her son.

Veronica didn't say anything. She just let herself be held. She was grateful that Christine had showered her that morning. Comforted, she fell asleep.

After she dozed off, Sean did not stay long. He wasn't fond of Veronica's mother, and would have refused to stay at the house had he been invited. Jacqueline Thomas was not fond of him either, especially as he had impregnated her daughter without a marriage proposal, and had no intention of inviting him to stay.

Sean went back to the flat that had been the happy home he shared with Veronica and their son.

Veronica stayed with her parents in her childhood room, afraid to go home to the absence of Jacob.

Seven days later, Christine returned. She showered Veronica again, stripped her bed, laid her down in fresh pyjamas and clean sheets, and presented her with a gift. It was a large box wrapped in silver paper and tied with a black bow.

'I really hope you like it but I will totally understand if you don't want it or think it is freaky. It might really help you, but if you think it would hinder you then I will take it away and we will never speak of it again,'

Christine said, sounding nervous. This was making Veronica more intrigued as she carefully took the wrapping off the package.

'It is the latest gimmick. You give them a photo and they make it look exactly the same,' Christine told her. Veronica opened the box. She sat there, not saying a word, just staring at her gift in the box. Unable to believe her eyes she tried to absorb what she was seeing.

'It looks so real, right? Do you see, it is the spitting image of Jacob. The skin feels real and warm. Feel it. Do you like it? If you hate it that is okay but I just thought it might help you get through this transition phase,' Christine told her, paranoid now that she might have overstepped. Veronica was still staring, speechless, at the life-sized realistic baby doll which was the spitting image of the four-month-old baby she had recently lost to cot death.

'Do you hate it? Please say something!'

'I love it!' Veronica said, reaching into the box and retrieving the warm baby doll into her needy arms. Milk from the swollen breasts leaked through her T-shirt.

'It doesn't talk or move on its own or anything. I didn't want anything that would freak you out but it opens and closes its eyes and pees just like those baby dolls we used to have as kids. You can feed it milk and it just goes straight into its nappy. So remember you need a nappy on it before you feed it. What makes it unique is that it is warm and the skin feels real, and yours looks exactly like Jacob.'

Veronica did not say anything. She just continued to stare down at the baby doll in awe. 'I picked up some nappies and baby clothes from your flat when I went to visit Sean. Sean seems to be doing okay by the way,' Christine told her, placing a bag of baby stuff on the bed.

Veronica said nothing; she just continued to stare at the lifelike doll.

'Right, I'm going to go then. I have a few things to do, and I also have to get home to feed Charlie,' she said, referring to her cat as an excuse to leave. 'Bye then!' She planted a kiss on the top of Veronica's head.

'Chris,' Veronica finally said, just as her friend was walking out the door.

'Yes?' Christine asked, turning back to her friend, somewhat relieved that Veronica had remembered how to communicate.

'Thank you.'

CHAPTER THREE

Veronica awoke the next morning with the warm baby doll in her arms. She smiled and kissed its head, feeling happier than she had in two weeks.

'Good morning, sunshine,' she said to Jacob's replacement. She hopped out of bed to put a fresh nappy and clothes on her new acquisition. Then placing the baby doll safely between two rolled up towels, she took herself off to the bathroom to shower and apply makeup.

Once dressed and ready for a new day, she scooped up the replica baby and went downstairs.

'What is that?' asked Jacqueline, horrified.

'For now, this is Jacob,' Veronica told her matter of fact.

'No Vero! That will not help you recover. You must accept the situation and move on,' Jacqueline told her.

'You deal with it your way! This is already helping, and I am moving on. I am going home today,' Veronica replied, collecting the rest of her stuff, and heading out the front door with the new Jacob.

Sean was overjoyed to see her walk through the front door but a little terrified when he saw she was carrying a baby. His first thought was that she had stolen a baby from the park or a hospital.

'Christine got him for me. Isn't he amazing! It has helped a lot of people in our position. Like a therapy doll,' Veronica explained.

When Veronica showed him the doll's face he was taken aback.

'Jesus Vero!' Sean said, and the tears started to flow.

'It will help us! Hold him. It is so comforting,' Veronica stated, placing the baby in his arms. He stared down at it. He didn't feel comfort, he felt like throwing up.

'I can't, Vero! This is not my son! If it helps you I am glad, but I can't play into this fantasy of yours,' he said, passing it back to her. The doll gave him the creeps but he did not protest further as he was so happy to have

Veronica home, and she seemed almost like her old self which he had feared he had lost forever.

'Would you like a cuppa?' Sean asked.

'Yes please,' she answered, following him into the kitchen with the new Jacob against her chest. She was rubbing his back as if soothing him.

Veronica sat at the kitchen table, raised her T-shirt, moved her bra to the side, and placed the baby's open mouth over her exposed nipple. She waited for her tea while feeding her imaginary baby. Sean wanted to scream. While the kettle boiled, he stood there watching her, biting his nails. This felt so wrong but Veronica was actually smiling and seemed relaxed and joyful. In a way he felt almost jealous, and wished he could be fooled into believing his son was still alive. He wished the joy would return to his eyes like it shone in Veronica's.

They chatted about things that were going on with friends. Sean tried to ignore the doll that was pressed to his girlfriend's breast. Veronica leaned forward to get her tea.

'Ow!' she gasped.

'Is it too hot? Did you burn yourself?'

'No. He must have a sharp bit on his lips,' she replied, taking the doll out from under her T-shirt and running a finger across its lips. The lips were smooth. She laughed.

'How strange! It almost felt like he bit my nipple. I must have caught it on something,' Veronica explained. Sean frowned, wondering if this delusion would become unhealthy. Veronica placed the baby over her shoulder and rubbed its back to burp it.

'I am going to take him to the park this afternoon. I miss chatting with the other mums and watching the children play.'

'No Vero! They are all going to think you have lost the plot!'

'They will understand that it is for comfort. I think they will be happy for me. I couldn't bear to go to the park childless.'

'Veronica, you are childless! It is a doll for Christ sake! Play with it at home if you must but don't go out into the public with it!' Sean protested. Veronica stood up, angrily.

'I will do whatever makes me feel an ounce of happiness. This is helping me to get through the day! If you don't like it then I will go back to my mum's house,' she told him curtly.

JACOB

'Okay, okay! I'm sorry!' he said, drawing her into a hug with the stupid doll in the middle.

CHAPTER FOUR

It was a lovely sunny day. A stroll through the park was surely what the doctor would order. Veronica pushed the pram in front of her, returning smiles to people who jogged on by, or elderly folk who relaxed on the benches, reading or feeding the pigeons.

By the pond, she reached into the pram and picked up the baby doll who was swaddled in a blanket.

'Look, Jacob, look at the ducks,' Veronica said, pointing to the fowl swimming on the surface of the water. They sat by the pond for a pleasant moment, and then they carried on to the playground.

Three mothers that knew Veronica saw her approaching.

'Do you think she is babysitting for someone?' Jane whispered.

'Jesus, she's brave! If my baby died I don't think I could go near anyone else's baby for about twenty years. I mean, how long has it been? A month?' said Tania.

'Not even three weeks!' Stephanie told her.

Veronica waved, and carried on walking towards them. They waved back.

'Hi Veronica! How are you doing?' Jane asked, concerned.

'I am starting to feel a little bit better. It has been crushingly hard, you know.'

'I can't even begin to imagine,' Jane replied.

'Hi Veronica. And who is this?' Stephanie inquired, trying to get a peek at the baby.

'This is something new I am trying. Now don't judge me! You might not agree with this, actually I don't care because it is helping me, but this is my Jacob replacement doll,' Veronica informed them, and turned the doll around so they could see.

Jane almost screamed. She got such a shock to see that the doll had the exact same face as Veronica's dead baby.

'Wow! That's really realistic,' commented Tania, trying to hide her disapproval. Stephanie didn't say anything.

'You can't imagine what it is like to have your child suddenly gone from your life, the emptiness in your arms. This helps me with that. It gives me something to hold, to love on.

I have all this pent up love to give a baby and this doll gives me a therapeutic release,' Veronica explained in terms that she thought might convince them.

'Why don't you and Sean try for another baby?' Jane asked.

'Give her a chance! She only gave birth a few months ago,' Tania stated, trying to be kind and then cringed wondering if she had said the wrong thing.

'Sean doesn't want to have another baby straight away. He thinks we need time to grieve first.'

JACOB

'And you? Don't you feel you need time to grieve?' Stephanie asked Veronica.

'I can't. It is too much! I literally just wanted to die. Then my friend Christine gave me this Jacob doll yesterday, and already I feel so much better. Yesterday, I couldn't even get myself out of bed to shower. I had to have help like an invalid. But today I am in the park chatting with you guys so there is no question about it, this Jacob doll is doing wonders to help me heal.'

'But don't you think suppressing it and transferring your devotion onto a doll is unhealthy?' Stephanie asked.

'I know, Stephanie, it might not be the healthiest thing in the world but I think it is a damn sight healthier than spend every minute away wanting to slit my own throat!' Veronica answered, angrily.

'Sorry, but I think it is wrong on so many levels! Here, Veronica, take my shrink's number. She might be able to help you before you get attached to that doll in a clinically psychotic way!' Stephanie had tried not to open her mouth because once opened her honest opinions always came flooding out.

'Is that a doll?' asked Tania's daughter, coming up to them to see why voices were being raised. 'Can I play with it?'

'No!' Veronica answered flatly. She put Jacob back in the pram and stormed off, leaving those closed minded, judgmental, condescending women behind.

CHAPTER FIVE

As she pushed the pram back through the park, people smiled. Even without seeing the baby, people seemed happy to know there was new life there. It was a bizarre phenomenon how even though babies were born every day for the last six million years, they still bought joy to others. People would draw closer trying to get a peek at the bundle of cuteness. When she took the baby out of the pram and held it in her arms, an older woman would usually get close enough to start a conversation.

'How old is your baby?' asked an elderly woman with blue rinse hair, sitting down on the bench beside Veronica.

'Four months.' Veronica replied.

'Boy or a girl?'

'Boy. His name is Jacob,' Veronica told the smiling woman who believed the lifelike doll to be a real sleeping baby. Veronica laid him down in the pram, covered him with a blanket and hung a thin sheet over the pram to block out the sun.

'Mine are all grown now with families of their own. I had three girls and two boys, but the boys were always easier. I have six grandchildren now!'

'How lovely for you,' Veronica said, sitting back down on the bench.

'It is lovely being a grandmother. So much less stressful than being a parent; and now mothers have to work too! I don't know how they do it! Mind you, you do have washing machines and dishwashers and the internet, and disposable nappies, all of which cut down on time. Do you work?'

'I'm not working at the moment, but I was a

teacher. I will go back to teaching when Jacob gets a bit older.'

It was so nice to have this pleasant conversation filled with hope and dreams for the future. Veronica knew the whole atmosphere would have been so different, so morbid, cut short with polite excuses to leave, if she had told the woman the truth that Jacob was dead.

'Children are such a blessing! Appreciate them being small as it goes so fast,' the blue haired old woman advised her. Veronica nodded, and then they sat in a comfortable maternal silence for a while, watching children playing on the stretch of green.

'Well, I have to go if I don't want to miss my bus home,' said the woman, smiling, and easing herself up from the bench. 'I just needed to rest a moment, and see the baby. It was lovely to meet you and Jacob. Such a good baby! I hope to see you both again.'

'Yes, it was lovely to talk to you. Take care!' Veronica replied. She really didn't want the simple moment to end. Everything had been right with the world for the last few minutes. 'I really ought to be going too. Jacob will need his next feed soon.' The woman smiled her approval and patted Veronica on the shoulder. Then she toddled off towards the bus stop.

Veronica hummed happily as she pushed the pram back across the park.

A good looking man stopped to help her get the pram up the five steps in front of the block of flats. Veronica thanked him. People were so kind when you had a baby.

'Hi babe,' called Sean when he heard the front door open. He stepped from the kitchen out into the dark corridor to greet her. He frowned a little when he saw Veronica with

Jacob's pram which reminded him of Veronica's temporary madness, but she looked happy so he didn't say anything.

'We had a lovely time in the park, didn't we Jacob?' she said. The doll opened its eyes as she lifted it out of the pram. 'Oh good, you are awake. Time for a feed and a nappy change, my beautiful boy,' Veronica cooed. Sean tried to ignore it, and went back into the kitchen.

'I'm making pasta, babe. It will be ready in ten minutes. Do you want a glass of wine?' Sean called to Veronica who was changing the doll in the baby's room.

JACOB

'No thanks sweetie, I still have to breastfeed Jacob,' came the reply. Sean sighed.

CHAPTER SIX

The doll was lying on the changing table with a fresh nappy on. Its eyes were open. Veronica picked him up and sat down in the rocking chair to feed him. She held him out in front of her for a moment, one hand supporting his head, the other under his back, the two tiny feet pressed against her chest. Strands of her hair had got caught in his tiny fist.

'Are you pulling mummy's hair? You little rascal! You mustn't pull mummy's hair,' she cooed in a soft voice. All of a sudden the tiny first opened, grasped a thick lock of her hair and pulled. Veronica screamed. Not from the pain of the hair pulling but from the fright of what had just happened but she did not drop the doll or throw it away from her.

'What happened?' asked Sean, running into the room.

'Oh nothing,' Veronica replied. 'Just thought I saw a spider, that's all,' she lied.

'Dinner is ready,' he said, relieved.

'Okay, I'm coming,' she replied, placing the baby doll down in the crib. She turned on the musical mobile above the crib, and gave the doll a last look, saying 'You be good now,' as she quietly closed the door.

They had a pleasant meal together. Sean talked about his work at the architect firm, and made her laugh with antics the other architects got up to in the office. It made him happy to see her laugh again, to see the shine back in her eyes.

Veronica did have a small glass of white wine to accompany the delicious shellfish tagliatelle he had made. After dinner, they washed and dried the dishes together. It was all going so well, they were a little bit tipsy, the soft music was romantic, and they started to make out. Veronica pulled away suddenly, and listened. She swore she had heard Jacob crying.

JACOB

'I better go and check on Jacob,' she said, and walked away to the nursery. Sean wanted to yell after at her to face facts but he let her go. He didn't want to crush her spirit at the end of this nice evening but he slumped down onto the sofa feeling crushed himself. He could hear Veronica singing lullabies to that monstrosity of a doll. The tears streamed down his face.

CHAPTER SEVEN

She could hear Jacob crying. She pulled back her side of the duvet, quietly got out of bed, and slipped her feet into her slippers.

As Sean was an architect, it had fallen to him to design their new flat which they had purchased together when they found out that Veronica was pregnant with Jacob.

Veronica had loved Sean's modern designs in the beginning but now she was really regretting agreeing to the design of the long domineering corridor. Sean had covered the walls and ceiling in large thin square slabs of black slate with spotlights sparsely placed in the long dark ceiling.

The contrasting floor was a path of long rectangular granite tiles in the palest ochre to give a reflection of light in the very dark, almost ominous looking, corridor.

The baby room was at the very end but the door was not visible from the beginning of the corridor, and in turn the beginning of the corridor was not visible from the end.

When entering the corridor from the kitchen or living room, the door at the end was completely absorbed into the darkness. It had an impressive but unnerving feel to the design. Sean had described it as minimalist chic with an expensive but slightly dangerous vibe. Veronica had been impressed that you could say all that with just title and positioned lighting and the genius creative mind which the father of her child had.

The doors to all the rooms were hidden in the slate tiles. There was a handle on the dark blue door at the end of the passage - the baby's room - framed in a dark blue grey, but all the other less obvious slate doors work on a push system and they revolved round to allow access into each room of the flat. The corridor looked elegant and powerful as it flowed through the centre of the flat leading off to every room. At night it was creepy. From the baby's end you couldn't see the front door as the optical illusion made it merge into the black. All you could see from the far end was the white antique pram that was parked just on the edge of the darkness.

They had cut the expensive floor tiles too short at the factory for the width of their corridor. Sean did not cut more of the same tile. He explained to Veronica that he did not want to make it look as if he had tried to fill the space. He wanted it to look like he had purposely done it to use the space.

Sean was torn between a dark blue almost black cement gully for a chic look or a lighter blue grey tile to make it pop.

He tastefully bought the blue grey tile to line the gully on the left that had a small drainage hole between the kitchen and front door. Sean told Veronica that if the kitchen or bathroom ever flooded, both being either end on the left, the water would drain off into the blue grey gully, and not leak into the bedrooms.

JACOB

The corridor gave Veronica the creeps at night even with the lights on, so she kept her eyes on the blue grey gully guiding the way on her left. She tried not to look up to see the optical illusion at the end of the corridor where the end had merged with the darkness and disappeared. It had always freaked Veronica out to think that her baby was in that invisible room, hidden behind the curtain of darkness.

However, inside the room was a delight of fresh white walls and white furniture with an out-of baby-reach window that was framed by thin white muslin curtains and the leafy trees outside.

She heard the crying getting louder and looked up. The corridor seemed to stretch away from her. Jacob sounded hysterical. She started running but the corridor kept on stretching, an endless passage towards the darkness. She ran faster.

All of a sudden, the dark blue was imposingly right in front of her. She reached down and turned the handle.

The brightness of the white room blinded her for a second. She didn't turn on the main light as it was weirdly as bright as mid afternoon inside the room.

JACOB

Jacob was lying in his crib screaming, waving his arms and legs about with tiny clenched fists, going puce in the face.

Without questioning it, Veronica went to him and lifted him to her chest to comfort him. She sang softly and rubbed his back. Jacob became quiet. She carried him over to the rocking chair, and sat with him; exposing her breast for him to feed. He latched on and massaged out the milk with his strong gums and pumping sucks. Veronica relaxed and enjoyed the feeling, a feeling that her maternal body craved. She sang soft lullabies and stroked his head.

He looked up at her with eyes so dark that they seemed to have no iris only big black pupils, like black holes in space, the light entered the centre of the iris and was never seen again. Veronica stopped looking at him, chose just to enjoy the feeling of having him leaning against her but not really looking. She was overlooking. She rocked with him.

'What are you doing?' Sean asked, sleepily walking into the dimly lit room with tasselled hair.

The image in the lamp light of his girlfriend's breasts spraying milk all over the freaky doll in her arms which was meant to resemble his son was enough to wake any man.

'What are you doing? It is the middle of the night! You don't need to be doing that anymore. You can get your rest now.'

'Jacob was crying hysterically!' Veronica told him.

'I didn't hear any crying, just you waking me up by not being there. I can feel when you are gone from the bed, and I heard you singing. Come on, baby. Put him down now, and come back to bed,' Sean guided, wiping her down with a wet wipe.

'Here, give him to me,' Sean suggested. 'I will clean him up and put him down.' Veronica carefully passed the now sleeping baby to him.

'You go back to bed. I will do this,' Sean insisted. Veronica kissed her baby on the head, said, 'Night, night Jacob,' and then she returned to bed, and switched on the baby monitor by her pillow.

Sean wiped the doll over as if cleaning a lifeless latex doll. Then he tossed it into the crib, turned off the lamp and left the room, closing the door behind him.

JACOB

'Turn the lamp back on in the baby room please!' Veronica ordered Sean when he reached their bedroom. It was too late at night to argue, so he went back to turn on the lamp.

He walked the corridor towards the thickening darkness. Sean opened the door to a black, black room. He felt his way through the cold blackness, and he finally found the lamp.

The baby doll climbed up the bars of its crib. The second the light went on, the life-like baby flew at him. Sean fell backwards onto the floor, smacking his head on the corner of a chest of drawers on the way down, resulting in a bloody cut.

Veronica had heard the thud and came running. The doll was laying innocently doll-like still in the crib.

'Are you alright?' Veronica asked, concerned. She helped him to get up.

'Yes! I thought I saw something, but it is just my imagination playing tricks because you keep making me paranoid with all this doll bullshit! Our son is dead, Veronica! When are you going to accept that? When are you going to be there to go through the grieving stage with me? Huh? Fuck this!' Sean yelled, angrily, and he stormed off to their bedroom where he got dressed, and packed a suitcase.

JACOB

'Where are you going?' Veronica asked in a slightly hysterical tone; all she could feel was panic.

'I'll go and stay with my parents until I sort this out,' he told her. She clung to his clothes.

'No! Please don't go! Don't leave me!' Veronica sobbed.

'I can't stay in the flat with that stupid doll any longer. You have to chose, Vero!'

'No, please stay,' she cried, grasping at his clothing, refusing to let go. He picked up the bag and tried to prize her off. She held on tight, begging. He walked to the front door dragging her with him.

'GET OFF ME!' he shouted when his foot had overstepped the threshold. It was so loud with an echo that she let go in fright. Sean gave her a light push to move her back inside and slammed the door closed.

CHAPTER EIGHT

It was quiet now in the flat, a defending silence filled all the rooms. Veronica felt too fragile to walk towards the darkness to check on Jacob.

She went and curled into ball on her bed. It felt so empty without Sean in it. She built a wall of pillows behind her, and sobbed herself to sleep.

In the subtle glow of the low watt lamp, Jacob crawled slowly across the floor of the baby's room. The door opened by itself with a low creak as it opened.

Jacob scuttled at super speed along the granite and slate corridor, pushed the door that swivelled, clawed his way up the bed, and lay curled up against mummy's warm tummy, sucking his thumb.

Veronica woke up holding the rigid doll. She couldn't remember waking up to get him but she must have. She looked down at him and she saw something she hadn't noticed before. The doll had two front milk teeth at the bottom just broken through the gum. That was a cute touch she thought.

JACOB

'Aww! Cutie Pie! Are your little toothy pegs growing?' Veronica cooed at the baby doll. She sat the baby up and its eyes opened, and then it began to cry, mechanically. Veronica thought that obviously Christine had forgotten to tell her about the crying feature.

Veronica latched the doll's open mouth over her nipple. The doll began to quietly suck with a mechanical pumping action.

Veronica wished now that she had not been so quick to throw away the booklet that had come inside the box with her Jacob doll. She wondered if there were any other features that Christine had neglected to mention, and

Veronica was now upset that she had failed to read in the booklet.

Veronica sat back and relaxed as the baby suckled. It was an indescribable feeling of comfort and nurturing, and a turn on. Veronica closed her eyes. Her nipples were hardening and it was starting to ache between her legs. It was just a doll not a real baby she reminded herself, conveniently.

The ache was getting stronger. She wet her fingers in her mouth and slid them into her knickers to relieve herself. As her body jolted from the rapid circling of her fingers, the doll's mouth stayed latched onto her breast but its body slid slowly down so that its foot now reached her clitoris. The sucking on her nipple got harder. Her circling became more frantic, its foot now resting in that gyrating hand, its toes pinching at her clitoris. Again she reminded herself that it was a lifeless doll not a real baby. This was not a sin, this was not damaging to another human being.

She looked down at the doll. Those black eyes fixed on her almost with a seductive knowing look that no baby should ever have. Her circling fingers were making her peak at that moment, and in the throes of an immense orgasm she could not stop her circling fingers that were clenched together in a spasm of muscle memory. The doll looked up as it began to crawl backwards down her stomach, a devilish look in its eyes, the mouth slightly twisted into a seductive grin.

Veronica watched it was a few seconds crawling backwards but as its mouth lowered towards her vagina, she screamed and flung the doll away from her. It hit the floor with a thud.

The doll turned its head with a creak to give Veronica a dirty look. Veronica noticed that another two milk teeth had grown up the top of the dolls mouth and they were disproportionately large. The doll smiled, and

Veronica could see all the teeth now burst through the gums and forming into full set of teeth with points at the end like a terrifying anglerfish.

The doll leapt from the floor, and raced towards her at inhuman speed. Before she could react, it latched onto her nipple, sucked super hard and fast and then feasted its way through the fat of her breast. Blood was spurting everywhere. Veronica was screaming. The red blood soaked into the white sheets as the monstrous doll devoured her left breast. Veronica tried to fight it off but it was unnaturally as strong as a full-sized demon.

CHAPTER NINE

Veronica woke up in a panic but she was fine. It must have been a horrifying dream which had left her feeling tainted and sinfully dirty.

Jacob was not in the room. She went down the dark corridor to check; fear paced back and forth in the cage hidden inside her chest.

The doll was lying quiet and lifeless in its crib where she had left it the night before. She laughed at herself and her silliness; but she went alone to the kitchen to have a relaxing cup of tea and a cigarette - now that Sean had left she may as well. She had a sneaky packet hidden in the linen cupboard under the pile of fresh smelling sheets.

She made a cup of tea, and sat down at the kitchen table with an ashtray to enjoy a sinful cigarette. She could hear the doll crying but she ignored it. There was the loud buzz of the doorbell. The crying stopped.

It was Christine at the door. Veronica let her in, and then refilled the kettle.

'You forgot to tell me that the doll cries,' Veronica scolded her friend playfully.

'Does it? Is it awfully annoying?' Christine asked, apologetically.

'Sometimes, like in the middle of the night.'

'Surely there is an off button somewhere,' Christine reasoned.

'I don't think so. I haven't found one. I stupidly threw away the booklet before reading it.'

'I don't really know much about it either. I didn't read the booklet. I was sold at the fact that it was going to be warm and cuddly and look like Jacob,' Christine admitted.

'Sean left! We weren't seeing eye to eye on things,' Veronica told her matter of fact.

JACOB

'Jesus, Veronica! I'm so sorry! Are you okay? It wasn't because of the doll, was it? What is that sound? Is that crying?' the questions were tumbling out of Christine's mouth and Veronica did not get time to answer them.

'I don't know!' were the words Veronica chose to cover all of her friend's questions. They listened out, and heard the crying again.

'It sounds realistic, just like a live baby! It's a haunting sound, don't you think?' Christine commented.

'No I find it really comforting, especially when I look in the room and there is something warm in the crib that I can pick up. I have improved a lot since you bought me that doll,' Veronica told her sincerely. She didn't tell Christine about the times it had frightened the life out of her.

'I'm going to the bathroom. Maybe you could shut that crying up?' Christine suggested, leaving the room. Actively ignoring the demanding sound, Veronica went to her bedroom to change out of her nightdress.

Christine was craving a biscuit to go with her tea, and returned to the kitchen to find the doll sitting in Jacob's highchair, wailing. She assumed Christine had placed it there.

'Hush now baby, don't cry, Auntie Christine is going to see if she can find you a biscuit in one of these cupboards. The doll stopped crying. Christine laughed, amused at the coincidental perfect timing.

A long glass, partially filled with water, slid from the counter and smashed on the floor into large jagged pieces. Christine turned to look, slipped on the water and fell to the floor. A large jagged piece of glass penetrated through her vital internal organs. Christine gurgled on her own blood as she tried to call out for help.

'Did you break something?' Veronica asked as she came into the kitchen, not expecting to receive such a bloody scene. She slid to the floor beside her friend, cutting her knees but not caring.

Assessing that her friend's wounds could be fatal, Veronica reached for her phone on the table, and called for an ambulance, urging them to come quickly, but it was already too late.

CHAPTER ELEVEN

Sean came to the funeral to pay his respects, and to see how Veronica was coping. Veronica found that the funeral service and seeing Sean were too much for her, so she left before the reception at Christine's mother's house which Veronica had helped cater for.

Veronica went back to the quiet empty flat where the silence was painfully loud. She curled up with a book and a cup of tea in the window seat of the living room's bay window, but she was distracted, watching the rain which had started to drizzle down, distorting the images of the old trees into ghostly figures on the other side of the wet glass.

She got up and went to the baby's room. She placed Jacob on the changing table and put on a fresh nappy, and a clean onesie that did not have splatters of blood on it.

She had not spent time with Jacob since Christine's accident. She had needed chrysalis time to herself. Now, with her emergence from the murky depths of sorrow, she found Jacob's presence comforting as he lay there on the changing table with his eyes closed.

JACOB

She picked him up, supporting his head and looked closely at the replica Jacob, wondering if the doll had anything to do with Christine's death; wondering if she had made the doll possessed by putting so much energy into it, or if Jacob's spirit had returned to her through the doll.

The storm clouds gathered in the bright white sky outside the window. Veronica's eyes started to roll back in her head. The baby kicked out and squealed, delighted by the whites of her eyes. He reached out, grabbing at strands of her dangling long blonde hair.

Lightning lit up the sky which had now turned dark and moody. Thunder rolled, and so did the eyes of Veronica Thomas.

'Mama,' said the baby sitting up, exposing a mouth full of lethal teeth. It reached forward yanking on her hair.

'MAMA!' Veronica did not verbally respond as she was convulsing, her eyes still rolling back in her heard.

'**MAMA!**' roared a demonic voice from the baby's mouth. The baby leaned forward and bit down hard on Veronica's arm. Veronica screamed, and came out of her trance. A loud roll of thunder sounded as the heavens tore open.

Veronica nursed her bleeding arm, and bandaged it. She then picked Jacob up and put him back in his cot.

Jacob did not like that. He was hungry and wanted feeding. When her back was turned, Jacob climbed the bars. She turned around and Jacob sprung onto Veronica's chest. In fright she threw him off. He pounced on her again, trying frantically to latch onto her left nipple, tearing through her clothes to find it. Again she threw him off but like a cat he sprung back, latched onto her nipple and sucked hard and fast. It hurt. Veronica tried to pull him off but he had her nipple between his sharp teeth and the more she pulled, the closer she came to tearing her nipple off. She tried to hit the doll with a heavy book of fairytales that she was able to reach on the shelf. She thumped it several times but the doll did not react, it just kept on sucking harder and harder. Veronica was crying out in pain.

Veronica ran to the kitchen with the doll still attached to her. She went to grab a kitchen knife but the doll was quicker, and it plunged the blade deep between her ribs and twisted it.

JACOB

The life-like baby doll yanked the knife out, wiped it on Veronica's clothes, put it back in its slot in the knife holder, and climbed up into his highchair to watch Veronica bleed out and die.

That is where Sean found the doll, in the baby highchair in the kitchen, seemingly looking down at Veronica's dead body on the kitchen floor.

After the forensics had been, and the coroner had taken away Veronica's body, Sean took the doll down to the street and threw it in the dumpster.

Later that evening, Sean had to go and give a statement, and was arrested on suspicion of the murder of Veronica Thomas. He had no alibi but he did have a motive, having broken up with her recently and the stress of losing a child which could have pushed him over the edge. The police had no other suspects so he was kept in custody for six months on remand, then tried, but acquitted on lack of sufficient evidence.

Meanwhile, a tramp had found the lifelike doll in the dumpster. It seemed such a waste to be thrown in the trash, so he walked a couple of

JACOB

blocks, and left the baby doll on the back step of the home for orphaned girls.

CHAPTER TWELVE

It was Sally that found it, much to her delight.

'What's your name?' Sally asked the doll. She heard the name Jacob in her mind. She liked it and decided not to change it.

'Hello, Jacob. Are you an orphan too? You can be mine now, and I will take care of you,' she told the lifelike baby doll, rocking it in her arms.

Sally thought the doll was beautiful but it was a shame that the dirty onesie had dark reddish brown stains splattered on it. In the bathroom, she tried to scrub the onesie clean

JACOB

with some soap but the stains wouldn't come out. So she kept the baby semi-naked, just wearing the nappy it came in, until she could find a way to steal a clean onesie from the babies ward.

Sally was seven, alone without friends or siblings, and having something to care for did her the world of good. To the jealousy of the other girls, Sally took her new baby with her everywhere.

'That doll looks like a really ugly freaky baby!' Caroline snarled at her in the cement yard behind the orphanage where the children were allowed to play.

'Don't listen, Jacob. You're not ugly! You are a beautiful baby,' Sally told the doll sleeping in her arms.

'Let me see it!' demanded Caroline.

'No!' Sally argued. Caroline grabbed it by the arm and pulled it away from Sally and held it up to inspect it.

'You can't even tell if it is a girl or a boy! It's just an ugly freak!' Caroline stated. Her two best friends, Tara and Mary, came over.

'It's a boy! His name is Jacob,' Sally yelled.

'How do you know the freak is a boy? Does it have a willy?' Caroline goaded, ripping off its nappy.

'Don't!' screamed Sally.

'Oh my god, it does have a willy! And look, its eyes open when you move it about,' Caroline told her friends who laughed as she shook it backwards and forwards. The doll peed on her.

'Err! The freak peed down my arm!' Caroline cried, throwing the doll to the ground. The dolls eyes opened and looked menacingly at Caroline. Sally leapt up, grabbed the doll, and comforted it. She put the nappy back on.

Now that it was secured in a nappy and unable to pee on her with what Caroline presumed was water, Caroline grabbed the doll again.

'Let's play Sally in the Middle with the freak,' Caroline ordered, throwing the doll to Tara who threw it to Mary. Mary missed it and the doll fell down hard on the concrete. Sally was crying, and tried to swoop in and save Jacob but she wasn't quick enough. Mary threw the doll to Caroline. Sally jumped as Jacob flew over her head.

JACOB

Just as Jacob was falling down into Caroline's outstretched hands, chunky green puree poured from its mouth down onto Caroline's face. It wasn't a lot but enough to repulse Caroline who threw the doll at Sally in disgust, and stormed off with her friends.

Sally looked at the doll in awe and wondered what else it could do.

It wasn't long before she found out.

CHAPTER THIRTEEN

Under the watchful eye of Sister Dolores, they all said their prayers on their knees, then crossed themselves and climbed into their beds.

Sister Dolores turned off the lights. Sally curled up under the coarse sheet and blanket with Jacob. She kissed him goodnight and stroked his head.

Content, Sally drifted off quickly into a heavy slumber, and the baby doll slipped quietly out of her bed.

It crawled along the floor and slid under the next bed. It waited and it watched.

JACOB

Sliding out from under the bed, it slithered on its belly to the next bed and slid under it. It moved slowly down the room under the beds.

Poppy's bed was empty because she was in the sickbay with a fever. Jacob slid to it, and clawed his way up onto Poppy's bed. Jacob looked over to the next bed where Caroline was sleeping.

Taking hold of the corner of Poppy's thick pillow, Jacob leapt onto Caroline's bed and covered the sleeping child's face with the pillow, pushing down hard. Caroline tried to struggle, she convulsed a little but it was all over pretty quickly with hardly any noise, not enough to wake the others who often heard louder thrashing when one of them had a nightmare. This was a common occurrence so they had learnt to sleep through it.

Jacob leapt with the pillow back to Poppy's bed where he replaced it. Then he slid down onto the floor, and slithered back under the beds to Sally. Jacob clawed its way up her bed and slid under the sheet, back into Sally's arms.

The next morning, the orphanage was in a ruckus. Sister Dolores had walked over to

Caroline's bed to demand she get up but had found the child grey and very dead.

The police were called in, and the children were kept off school because they all needed to be interviewed.

The children gathered in the yard were in brouhaha or crying. Sally wasn't crying. She was sitting quietly with Jacob in the tire swing, thinking how glad she was that Caroline could no longer subject her to mêlées in public.

Sally was not at all sad that Caroline was dead. As long as she had Jacob, Sally was happy.

CHAPTER FOURTEEN

Caroline's death became unexplained mystery that everyone gossiped about.

No actual charges were brought against anyone despite the police bringing all the Sisters in for heavy questioning. Sister Dolores was kept three hours longer than the rest, and was interviewed in a different room.

The police figured that none of the other children were strong enough to hold a pillow down over Caroline's face for long enough with Caroline fighting them off. All the other children were smaller and weaker than

Caroline who had been the largest child at the orphanage. At fifteen, she had stood five foot seven inches and she was a heavy girl.

Caroline's mental age had not been fifteen. She had learning difficulties and had the personality of a delinquent twelve-year-old.

Caroline's best friends, Tara and Mary who were both twelve, had wailed in anguish at the loss of their friend. The other girls only cried as death was an emotional occurrence but none of them would miss Caroline with her big gob and mean personality.

The sadness at the orphanage only lingered for a week. It was replaced by rumours and conspiracy theories which turned into ghost stories that kept all the girls awake at night.

Sally carried on as before, feeling safer than she had ever felt. Tara and Mary didn't bother her. Now that their gang leader was gone, so was their confidence.

At the end of the month, the girls had their minds distracted by the Find a Family Day that was coming soon. There was talk of the orphanage being closed while investigations continued, and so the Sisters were eager to find homes as quickly as possible for the children. Those that did not find homes would be put in foster care. No one wanted to be put in foster care, like a hired car that was going to be loved for a while but then returned one day slightly more damaged than before.

All the girls were twittering about what they were going to wear to impress the potential parents that were coming that day, and dreaming about the couple who would fall in love with them and take them home to a big beautiful house where they would have their own room, and no longer have to listen to Poppy coughing all night, and smell Tracey's funny farting.

Sally didn't care anymore if she got adopted. Life in the orphanage with Jacob was not too bad now. As long as she followed the rules about not running, eating all her greens, making her bed, saying her prayers, and doing her evening chores, the Sisters would not beat her, and life ran smoothly according to schedule. Sally saw no reason to change that or place her trust in others. A new mum and dad might be nice. If it happened - it happened, if it didn't - she wasn't bothered.

CHAPTER FIFTEEN

Many of the children had been complaining of being woken by the sound a baby crying. Their dormitory was too far from the baby wing to hear any of the babies, but night after night several of them heard the wailing baby.

There was a rumour spreading through the orphanage like a contagious rash, that one of the babies had died and its ghost was now living in the walls of the orphanage. The children concluded that is what had killed Caroline. It could come for anyone of their souls any night. Hardly anyone slept anymore.

Sally only fed Jacob water which kept soaking his nappy so she had to dry it out and take Jacob around with her with his penis exposed, so of course she got teased by the others.

Whenever she got the opportunity, she stole nappies from the baby wing during lunchtime or sometimes during the night.

She had taken Jacob with her on these escapades and had shown Jacob the six cute babies sleeping in their cribs.

There was a large tin of milk formula on the shelf. Sally poured some into her pocket, and stole four nappies from the pile.

The night crying that had haunted the children had been Jacob wailing uncontrollably with hunger, but now he knew where he could find food.

Sally used the milk powder sparingly mixed with a lot of water, so at night the hungry doll slithered out of her bed, head first, and crawled across the floor and under the beds.

It crawled down the dark corridors, quiet and stealth-like, animalistic and predatorily, towards the room of babies.

It stood on its two legs and looked at the babies in the cribs. It decided on the smallest one, a slightly premature but healthy newborn that had been found the day before in a large refuse container.

The replica baby climbed up into the cot with the newborn. Jacob placed his little hands around the smaller baby's tiny neck and squeezed as hard as he could. The neck snapped.

JACOB

Taking the dead baby's arm in his mouth Jacob scaled the bars of the crib, up and over with ease, dragging the small corpse with him. It crawled through the darkness along the corridor dragging its prey all the way to the bathroom.

Jacob threw the dead baby into the toilet; and then leapt up onto the seat of the toilet where he sat squatting on his haunches, dipping into his feast of baby soup.

Claws extended from his latex fingers, he tore off the babies flesh, and devoured it with fervour. Blood spurted in the bowl and coloured the water red but the rest of the bathroom stayed clean. Jacob was pleased with the success of his deviously cunning dinner plan.

When he'd had his feed, he flushed the rest of the small baby down the toilet.

Jacob washed himself off in the clean toilet waterfall, dried himself on the hanging hand towel, and crawled back down the dark corridor to Sally's bed.

CHAPTER SIXTEEN

In their best clothes with smiles painted on their faces, the children wandered about the busy hall eyeing up the prospective parents who were going around chatting with the children they liked the look of.

All the potential parents had applied months in advance and gone through rigorous screening before this day.

A few of the prospective parents had been asked to wait in another room because each of these couples would be called into a meeting with Sister Benedict as they had been pre-matched to a child. This would be the date they would meet the girl that they were actually taking home at the end of the day.

The children who had been pre-matched had not been told. The establishment did not want to overexcite the children until they knew the new parents would show up, for fear of disappointing a child if they didn't.

Clare had fallen in love with their soon-to-be daughter as soon as she saw her photo. Since then she had talked about nothing else and was driving her new husband crazy, although he was looking forward to it too.

JACOB

Clare had known since she was twenty-five that she was infertile but she really wanted a child, and her new husband had lost a child during his previous relationship, so neither of them wanted to wait. It was something they both felt they needed. They knew this had bought them closer. Maybe this is why they got married so quickly, and almost immediately started the adoption process.

On their application, they had ticked that they would be open to adopt any child up to the age of ten. They wanted to be able to get to know and mould the child before they reach the difficult years of puberty.

Thinking that there was a chance that they might get an unnamed baby or an older child that wanted to change their name, Clare bought a book of names and their meanings.

'Why did you choose Jacob for your son's name?' Clare asked her handsome husband who was pouring her a glass of red wine.

'Veronica thought of it. It is a biblical name isn't it?' Sean replied. 'I liked the sound of it.'

'It says here in this book that Jacob means supplanter – to take the place or position of somebody by force or intrigue, especially if that someone is no longer relevant or is obsolete.'

'I never knew that. That is kind of creepy! Especially considering everything that happened to Veronica afterwards,' he said, passing her a glass of red wine.

They climbed the front steps nervously but excited, watching a lot of other prospective parents walking into the building ahead of them. They were so glad that they had been pre-matched and didn't have to fight over the cutest children with the rest of them.

They were asked to wait in the seated queue outside Sister Benedict's office. Clare was getting more and more nervous by the minute. They had to wait forty-five minutes, watching other couples go in, and another girl being paraded through the room of impatiently waiting overly excited new parents.

'And how long have you been married?' Sister Benedict asked them, shuffling the papers on her desk, and then peering at the couple over her half-moon spectacles.

'Oh not long, but we were friends all through school, girlfriend and boyfriend through college. Then we separated for three years, and Sean had a child with someone else; but the child died. His relationship didn't work after that, and so we got back together and we both want a child as soon as possible,' Clare told the Sister.

'And you are happy to adopt a seven-year-old? Actually she is almost eight now. She was quite a sad child for the first few years she was here; but about nine months ago she found a doll to love, and now she seems quite happy.

She's a sweet little thing with a lot of love to give,' Sister Benedict told them.

'Sally is her name, right?' Sean asked, enthusiastically.

'Yes. Sally Jenkins but she can take your last name if you like, but she is too old to have her first name changed now.'

'Sally's a nice name. I'm okay with Sally,' Sean stated.

'Ah! Here she is now,' said Sister Benedict, addressing Sally who was being shown into the room by Sister Mary who had just told Sally the good news. Sally had changed her mind about being adopted; having heard that the orphanage might close and she would be put into foster care.

'Hello, I'm Sally!' she said boldly with a cute cheeky smile. 'I was told that I'm going to be your new daughter!' she announced, holding out her right hand to shake theirs and holding Jacob behind her back with her left hand.

'That's right, Sally! We are so happy to have you,' said Sean, beaming and shaking her hand gently. She had a surprisingly tough grip for a little girl. Clare was nodding enthusiastically beside him and smiling.

'Oh, and this is Jacob,' Sally announced, holding up her prised possession. Sean's face dropped as the replica of his dead son's eyes fixed on him, malevolently.

'Where I go Jacob goes!' Sally insisted.